GW01007427

Good luck Kyle !

Best wishes,

THE BUNBURYS

The Tail of Two Kitties

Text by David English
Pictures by Jan Brychta

COLLINS
8 Grafton Street, London W1

In Memory of Wilf Slack

Dedicated to Eric Clapton,
Rose, Pat and Conor.

William Collins Sons & Co. Ltd.
London · Glasgow · Sydney · Auckland
Toronto · Johannesburg

First published in Great Britain 1989

Copyright © David English and Jan Brychta, 1989

BRITISH LIBRARY CATALOGUING IN PUBLICATION DATA

English, David, *1936–*
A tail of two kitties.
I. Title   II. Brychta, Jan
823'.914 [J]

ISBN 0-00-215327-0

Printed and bound in Great Britain by
Scotprint Ltd, Musselburgh

Several years had ticked by since Bunbury had walloped
Whiskertown in the Bunson & Hedges Cat West Final.

Chairman Miaow and his team captained by Geoff Boycat
were still smarting over the defeat.

So was the newly elected Whiskertown President, Ernest
Mogg, a ruthless industrialist who had made his fortune from Mogg
and Brass, a feat of which he continually reminded his colleagues.

Inside the committee room of the Whiskertown pavilion,
Ernest Mogg strutted up and down, paws clasped firmly behind
his back.

'We're not going to be humiliated by a bunch of bunnies.
I want revenge. What do you say Miaow?'

Slowly and with great dignity Chairman Miaow rose to his feet.
'I'm sorry, Mr Mogg, but we just don't seem to be good enough.'

'Not good enough!' stormed Mogg, beating the table,
'N-O-B-O-D-Y tells me we're not good enough. I want another

meeting here tomorrow night with firm suggestions, otherwise there will be a few scalded cats who will be shown the door. Understand?'

And with that Ernest Mogg turned and made his exit.

'Phew!' said Geoff Boycat. 'By gum, President's a bit oopset!'

The following evening, as the moon danced on the gasometers and the smoke trailed from the tapering chimneys of Whiskertown, the Cricket Committee racked their brains for a solution.

'We could always doctor the pitch,' piped up Chris Tabby-Ray.

'What I'm thinking is, we should sabotage their Bunnymobile. Take the Tiger out of the Tank so to speak,' suggested Imran Kitten with typical poise.

'I say we spike their lettuce and carrots,' said Pussy Cat Willis. 'Get 'em where it hurts most: in their bunny tummies.'

'Let's frame Buntham: make up some "porkypies" and flog them to the *Bun*,' said Mike Catting. 'They love an expawsé.'

'No! No! No!' sighed an exasperated Mogg fidgeting from one paw to another. 'It's all been done before!'

Then, pulling his gold watch from his waistcat pocket, he announced, 'My, is that the time! Come on, gentlemen. Time is money. I haven't . . .'

'You might have to spend some of that money, Mr President, if you really want to beat the Bunburys.'

Ernest Mogg had been cut short in mid-sentence. It was Professor James Whiskers.

The cats' eyes turned on him as he unfolded his plan.

'Brilliant, Professor! Brilliant!' boomed Mogg, banging the table, which promptly awoke three of the Committee, catnapping on their blotters.

'Come here, son.' Mogg took the Professor by the ear and marched him to the window overlooking the town. Proudly putting his arm around him, he said, 'One day, Professor, this will all be yours.'

'Thank you,' gasped the little genius, fighting for breath.

'I've always wanted a gasometer and six tapering chimneys.'
   Mogg didn't hear him. He just squeezed the Professor harder
and gazed out of the window.
   'Aye, I think we're going to whop those Bunburys!'

Back in Bunbury, the team was busy preparing the ground for the game against the Foxes from nearby Flowery Field.

'Higher, Beefy!' cried little Rajbun. 'Lift me higher!' Ian Buntham and Rajbun were painting the sightscreens. Rajbun was tiptoed on Buntham's shoulders, trying to reach the top.

'Hello, Beefy!' laughed Allan Ram, slapping Buntham heartily on the back. That's all it took. Poor Rajbun toppled backwards, spilling all the paint over Buntham's head.

'You baaaaa . . . ram! I'll cook you in mint sauce!' shouted a furious Buntham, covered in paint.

'Now now, Beefy, don't get overemulsional,' shrieked Ram, fleeing for his life.

'Come on, lads, settle down.' It was Old Holbun, stepping out of his cottage. 'Come over here. I've got some important information.'

One by one the Bunburys strolled over to hear their Manager's news. Dennis Lettuce had been bowling flat out to his great chum Rodney Munch in the nets.

'Jeepers, Denno, if you perform like that this afternoon, you'll sure have those Foxes twitchin'.'

John Emberbunny fastidiously spun the ball to his partner Phil Edbuns.

Graham Dillbunny was completing his fourth circuit of Bunbury Green. His bunny bone had been causing him trouble, and he was giving it some pre-match exercise.

'Come on, Viv,' called Philip de Fruit Bun. 'The old man wants us.' Viv was miles away, listening to his Bunny Walkman.

'Ya, man, just coolin' out to Brian Furry and Foxy Music to get into the right groove.'

Relaxing on the grass, the Bunburys listened to Old Holbun. 'Frances Edbuns has just rushed this morning's *Bugle* over to me. Take a look at the headlines.'

WHISKERTOWN SIGNS OVERSEAS STAR TO DEFEAT BUNBURYS.

E. MOGG PAYS FORTUNE FOR CARIBBEAN CAT — HATTRICK CATTERSON.

'Phew,' whistled Goldenhare Gower. 'Hattrick Catterson. He must be the cat's whiskers! Do you know him, Viv?'

'No, man,' replied Viv. 'Can't say I've heard of him.'

'So they've had to resort to an overseas player, eh,' pondered Old Holbun, pulling thoughtfully on his pipe. 'Mmm . . .'

'Anyway, first things first. We've got to outfox those Foxes. We'll face Mr Catterson later . . .'

'Just one more snap, Hattrick . . . Smile!'
Patrick Twitchfield and the papacazzi were at Catwick in full
force to meet Hattrick Catterson.
The Big Cat marched through the surging throng of admirers.

'I'm Gloria Bunniford from the Bunbury Broadcasting
Corporation. Just a few words please, Mr Catterson. Why have you
come to England?'
As he busily signed autographs, Hattrick looked up and

beamed. 'I've come to make Whiskertown the Top Cats. I intend to whop those Bunburys and send them hoppin'. I also wanna meet some cute kitties. What are you doin' tonight, baby?'

'Oh, Mr Catterson, really,' blushed Gloria.

And with that, Hattrick was ushered into a Catillac limousine and swept away in a blaze of tail lights.

As the crowd swarmed after the motorcade, Gloria was left, a solitary figure, to contemplate the arrival of the Whiskertown Messiah. 'Yes, Mr Catterson, you can ruffle my fur any time!'

Hattrick Catterson's appearance in Whiskertown had certainly created the desired effect. The team's change in fortune was uncanny. Everywhere it played Ernest Mogg paraded his prize pussession for all to see.

Whiskertown walloped the Weasels and hammered the Hamsters, and even Barking's Terry Doberman and its film-star Chairman Michael Canine finished as underdogs after a fierce tussle.

The
Daily Tail
MAGAZINE

KERTOWN POST

CATS

MOUSE
75 YEARS O

Catterson's progress had been carefully monitored by the Bunbury players.

'I don't know how he does it,' sighed Goldenhare. 'Hattrick Catterson never seems to go to bed. Look at this: "Out in the early hours again at London's swinging night spots."'

Goldenhare was pawing through the week's papers in the pavilion.

'Here he is with Eartha Kitten at the Hoppodrome . . . Friday it was the opening of *Cats* with Andrew Lloyd-Whisker; Saturday night all bushy tailed with Sam Fox; Monday, Agatha Friskie's *Mousetrap* . . . it goes on and on!'

Jack Rabbit Richards and Vic March Hare looked up from their cressword puzzle.

'And here he is in the *Daily Tail* with Maria Whitticat and Peter Stringbean.'

'And yet,' mused Old Holbun, 'he always seems to be in devastating form on the pitch the next day . . . Very strange.'

When the big day arrived you couldn't buy a ticket anywhere.

'Whiskertown versus Bunbury. Get your tickets here!' shouted the touts.

The Whiskertown Ground was packed as the Bunburys arrived at the WG Grass Gates.

'Straight through there,' grinned the gateman. 'I don't know why you bothered to come. You've got no chance.'

'Charming,' mumbled Buntham.

'Come on, Holbun. What will you have?' boomed Ernest Mogg in the committee room. 'Get him a drink, Miaow!'

'Hello, Chairman. It's good to see you again. I'll have a large carrot juice,' said the Bunbury Manager politely.

Holbun walked to the window with his old foe, and, out of Mogg's earshot, said, 'So, you've been playing extremely well.'

'Well, you could say that,' agreed Chairman Miaow. 'Holbun, there is something you should know . . . I . . .'

'That's enough of all the chit chat!' Miaow was stopped in mid-sentence as Ernest Mogg stepped in between the two rival managers.

'Let's take our seats, gentlemen. Game's about to start. Everything all right, Professor?'

Professor James Whiskers gave Mogg the thumbs up as Bunbury took the field.

Whiskertown had won the toss and elected to bat.

Geoff Boycat and Graham Pooch on loan from Barking CC made a steady start.

A ball from Dennis Lettuce whizzed through Boycat's whiskers, prompting Richie Bunaud to comment, 'And that one missed by a hare's breadth.'

Pooch, after some dogged resistance, was finally caught by
Viv Radish off a long hop.

This brought Mike Catting to the wicket, and he quickly
dominated the bowling in his usual pugnacious style. But it was
clear who the crowd had come to see.

'HATTRICK! HATTRICK! We want HAT . . .!' chanted the
spectators.

Bunny Johnston and Richie Bunaud rattled on furiously as E W
Bunson and Frances Edbuns typed away in the press box.

The Bunburys went up with an enormous appeal against
Boycat for LBW. Umpire Dickie Purred put his finger up and the
dejected Whiskertown skipper trudged off back to the pavilion.

'Old sour puss,' whispered Buntham to himself.

And there, shining on the top step, was Hattrick Catterson. Out
he strode to the middle, twirling his bat and grinning at the
Bunbury fielders with a fixed smile.

There was a breathless hush around the ground as Buntham
steamed into Hattrick from the Foxhall end.

Whack! The cat's reply was a colossal 6, sending the ball straight back over Buntham's head and clean out of the Ground.

Catterson proceeded to carve the Bunbury bowling to all parts, scoring a mighty 186. He would have continued, but a shower of rain sent the players scurrying off the field.

'He's like a bloomin' run machine,' moaned Buntham, towelling himself down.

'He looks a bit off colour to me,' remarked Edbuns.

Sure enough, the black cat had changed colour to become a ginger tom.

'What's wrong, Hattrick? Don't you like the rain?' enquired Emberbunny.

There was no reply from the superstar.

'He's a bit non-committal, isn't he?' said Goldenhare.

The shower subsided and Whiskertown declared their innings at 275 for 2.

As Goldenhare and Cress Broadbun prepared to face the first ball, Catterson marked out his long run-up.

'Do you want the screens moving to the right or left?' enquired umpire Bill Alley Cat.

'Neither,' said Goldenhare. 'How about between me and the bowler!'

Sparks flew as the cat ran in like an express train, his legs pumping like pistons. The ball scorched past Goldenhare's nose.

'Smell the leather, Bunbury Boy!' yelled the crowd.

As the wickets started to tumble, Old Holbun looked on from the pavilion. It was difficult to disguise his despair. 'I don't know. I just don't know,' sighed the Manager.

'What's wrong, Holbun? Can't you take a beating?' boasted Mogg.

It was then that Old Holbun spotted the headlines of the afternoon's paper.

HATTRICK CATTERSON TO OPEN NEW BRANCH OF HABICAT

Holbun examined the article closer. It said, 'Cricket Star to Open New Branch of Habicat in Mousewell Hill at 3.30 pm.'

Holbun had hardly looked up when Chairman Miaow caught his eye.

'One minute!' exclaimed Holbun. 'If Hattrick Catterson is in Mousewell Hill, who the hell is that out there?'

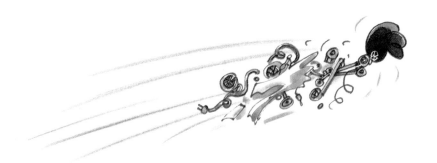

Before Chairman Miaow could explain, the rain started again. This time it was a summer storm.

Hattrick Catterson was striding to the wicket when he was suddenly struck by a flash of lightning. To the absolute astonishment of the crowd the cat lit up and his head flew off his shoulders. Little Rajbun who was facing the demon bowler almost fainted in amazement as the headless kitty continued to bowl.

As his arm came over, it left its socket and went flying through the air.

Crash! went the arm straight through the committee window, hitting Ernest Mogg smack on the head. It was now raining cats and dogs, but the players remained rooted to the spot, gaping in total disbelief as the cat exploded into a million fragments.

Frances Edbuns and her media colleagues were soon on the move. Quickly they entered the pavilion to demand an explanation.

Old Holbun was still in shock as Chairman Miaow unfurled his story: 'You see, the real Hattrick Catterson is quite an ordinary cricketer. Professor Whiskers made a mechanical cat, based on a bowling-machine principle, to resemble Catterson on match days.'

'Now it all makes sense,' said Holbun. 'No wonder his showbiz lifestyle didn't take toll. He had an identicat on the field. The purrfect crime!'

'Cat Bolts and Screws Game. Springs Recoil on Bent President!'

Frances Edbuns telephoned the news excitedly to her editor in Bunbury.

Amidst all the hubbub Ernest Mogg had slowly come round. Surrounded by police, he staggered to his feet, still dazed.

Just then, the door burst open. It was Hattrick Catterson with a Bunny girl on each arm.

'Just back from the Habicat opening. How's the game going, boss?'

Ernest Mogg didn't answer. For the second time that day the Whiskertown President was to collapse to the floor.

Hattrick Catterson was never to be seen again. As for his partner, he still remains in pieces – RIP (Rust in the Pavilion).

David English managed the Bee Gees and Eric Clapton before
becoming an actor. He has just produced his first
feature film with Barry Gibb, entitled *Hawks*.
He plays cricket for Middlesex CCC, the MCC, Cross Arrows CC,
Finchley CC and the EC XI. He first worked with
Jan Brychta presenting *You and Me* for the BBC.

Jan Brychta is a Czechoslovakian-born, award-winning artist
who has worked as a designer and illustrator on
a number of BBC television programmes for children,
such as *Jackanory, Play School* and *Music Time*.